To my **Maa**,
whose silent tears became the rain that grew me.
She never gave up—*na kabhi thaki, na kabhi ruki.*
In her quiet courage, I found my own.

To my **Papa**,
a man shaped by struggle, not softness—
Zindagi ne unhe kathor banaya, but beneath that stern
voice was a heart that carried the weight of us all.

To my **Bhai**,
my shadow, my strength,
who stood by me since childhood.
He held my broken days, lifted me through rejections,
and whispered, "*Tu kar sakti hai*,"
when I forgot to believe.

And to my **Didi**,
my first friend, my summer sky,
who left this world but never left me.
2017 ke baad duniya badal gayi,
but every phone call, every laugh, every village walk—
they still echo in my heart like a soft lullaby.
You were my cousin, but more—you were my home.

This book is for them—
the ones who made the dreamer in me dare to speak.
Each word here carries a piece of their soul.

Contents

Prologue

Whispers of a Dreamer's Heart
By Shweta Kanwar
    "Lily was a little girl, afraid of the big wide world..."
    Some stories don't begin with laughter.
Some girls don't bloom in the spring.
    This is the story of a quiet child—
soft eyes, softer voice,
and a heart that held more than it should.
    Lily didn't speak much,
not because she didn't have words,
but because the world had never learned
how to listen gently.
    She cried sometimes,
not in front of people—
but alone, under her blanket of stars.
    And she learned something rare:
that *crying is okay.*
That *some healing only comes in silence.*
That *a girl can break, and still find a way*
to glue her heart back with dreams.
    Her fear wasn't weakness.
It was memory—
and a body that remembered more than it was ever told.
    When life got too loud,
Lily turned to the sky.
She imagined clouds as boats,
fireflies as friends,
and poems as prayers.
    Her sister—her safe place—was now gone,
and yet Lily still walked barefoot through the summer

fields,
holding on to the echoes of laughter,
and the rustling sound of home.

She was a dreamer—yes.
But also,
a warrior with a heart made of soft storms.

This book is not a tale of grand victories.
It's about quiet bravery.
About crying when no one is looking.
About surviving without applause.

So, if you've ever felt unseen,
unheard,
or undone—
sit down beside Lily.

She's waiting to tell you
that healing is real,
and dreaming is enough.

ONE

A WHISPER IN THE DARK

A Father's Light

In the hush of rain, where shadows creep,
A child sat still, too scared to weep.
With skies turned grey and no one near,
Her little heart beat loud with fear.
But then, a sound—a distant hum,
A light that told her, "I have come."
Upon the road, through dusk so stark,
Her father found her in the dark.
No crown, no sword, no shining shield,
Just muddy boots and love revealed.
A warm embrace, a soft-lit face,
She learned that night: love finds its place.

She was barely five—tiny, soft, and scared of the unknown.

Lily had lived her earliest years in a mud house tucked in a quiet village where the nights whispered through oil lamps and the days began with the smell of woodsmoke and warm milk. There was no electricity when she was born, no running fan to cool her summer cries. Life was quiet, and dreams were woven in the dust under her feet.

Her village had a school, yes—but only until the eighth class, and learning there was slow, limited, dull. Her parents, though not wealthy, were wise. They knew the world beyond the mud walls was vast, and it held something greater for their daughter. So they enrolled her and her elder brother in a town school nearly 15 kilometres away.

Every morning, Lily and her brother boarded a bus—or more often, a *jugad*, that bumpy, makeshift village vehicle built from scrap but powered by hope. She would wake at 5 a.m., tie her small shoes, and hug her mother tightly before heading off at six, half-asleep and holding her brother's hand.

That rainy day changed something in her heart forever.

The skies had turned heavy, and the village roads became thick with mud. Halfway to town, the vehicle stopped—its wheels drowning in the brown sludge. One by one, the older boys and other children left, jumping into the muck, walking ahead through the storm. Her brother, just a little older, followed.

And Lily was left behind.

She didn't cry—not yet. She sat in silence, her small hands clutched around her schoolbag, her wide eyes looking out at the emptiness forming around her. The rain tapped against the tin roof like a ticking clock. It grew darker. She was too scared to move. Too young to know what to do.

But she waited.

And in the distance, through the mist and fading light, came the sound of a motorbike. She held her breath.

It was her father.

He had come for her.

Covered in mud, soaked from head to toe, his eyes found her, and in them, she saw safety. She ran into his arms, and that moment—drenched, dirty, but held close—felt like magic. She would remember that feeling every time she ever got lost again in life.

At home, her mother sat her on a clean cloth, wiped her face gently, and gave her a warm roti with ghee, jaggery, and sugar. The taste still lives somewhere in her memory, a flavour of being loved.

That night, Lily didn't sleep out of fear anymore. She slept hugging her small pillow, the one she never used for her head, but always held like a soft toy—a quiet, personal comfort.

And in her heart, a whisper remained:
"Even in the dark, someone will come for you."

TWO

THE WORD THAT BROKE HER SMILE

Sometimes the smallest cracks echo the loudest pain
In the hum of chalk and classroom air,
A little heart stood trembling there,
One word, one miss, one shameful glare,
And silence louder than despair.

Tiny fingers gripped her slate,
Eyes welled up with the teacher's hate,
She knew the letters, tried her best,
But kindness lost, failed the test.

On that dusty village ride back home,
Mocking whispers etched her own,
Yet in her heart, a fire stayed bright—
To learn, to rise, to rewrite her night.

The Word That Broke Her Smile

The school in town had glossy floors, crisp uniforms, and walls that echoed English words she barely understood. Lily, just four, sat near the front—nervous, shy, and silent. The letters danced in her small head every night, but under the gaze of her strict English teacher, they scattered like birds in a storm.

That day, the word was "elephant."

She had whispered it over and over to herself, her tiny lips brushing the pillow the night before, spelling it out with her fingers in the dark. Her mother had lit a dim bulb while preparing dinner in the mud kitchen; her brother, sitting beside her, had tried to help—but English wasn't easy for any of them.

And then, under the harsh white light of the classroom, when the teacher asked her to speak, her tongue faltered. Maybe it was an extra 'e'... maybe the 'ph' had gone missing. But whatever it was, it wasn't perfect.

The stick came down hard.

The sting on her hand wasn't as sharp as the sting in her heart. Her little body trembled. The room didn't gasp, didn't flinch. They were used to this. But Lily? She broke—silently.

No one noticed how long she stayed quiet after that. On the school bus back to the village, the other kids teased her: *"Elephant! Elephant! Even the baby can't spell!"*
The ride home, through fields and fading skies, felt longer than usual. She sat quietly, looking out at the vast world she didn't feel part of.

That night, her mother fed her warm rotis with ghee and jaggery. The same comforting hands that juggled studies and housework tried to soothe the ache her daughter didn't speak of. Her brother sat nearby, a silent witness, unsure how to protect her but trying to make her laugh.

In a small mud room where water still dripped through the thatched roof, her mother studied at night, sometimes by the flicker of just two bulbs, surrounded by the children she tutored for free. Lily watched her mother, eyes full of wonder and pain—how could someone so burdened still teach others to rise?

And slowly, in the shadows of a leaky ceiling and the hum of a struggling fan, a fire grew in Lily—not just to study, but to believe in herself when the world chose to embarrass her.

She picked up her pencil again.

THREE

WHEN THE WALLS BEGIN TO SHIFT

*"A flower raised in mud learns to bloom without asking the sky
for light."*
    They moved her roots but not her soul,
From fields of dust to city's scroll.
She held her breath through language storms,
And learned to fit in foreign forms.
    She walked alone, no hand to hold,
With aching limbs and stories untold.
But deep inside, she lit a spark—
A quiet flame that braved the dark.

    The village school's blackboard was chipped at its edges, and the wooden benches creaked like old secrets. By the time Lily reached Class 4, her eyes had grown used to the dusty chalk lines and the smell of midday sweat mixed with dried mud. The bus that once carried her and her brother had become unreliable—often broken, sometimes not arriving at all. So the siblings had started attending the village school instead, surrounded by their dialect, their soil, their silence.

But education in that school was a distant cousin of what her mother had imagined.

The teachers, though kind at times, were often absent. There weren't enough of them anyway. Lessons floated in the air but rarely entered the hearts of the students. Local language was the only bridge of communication, and Lily's world remained untouched by the languages beyond the hills—Hindi was rare, English a ghost.

Then came a letter. One dusty afternoon, a postman with cracked sandals handed her father an envelope with a government seal. Her mother had been selected for a teacher's training program in the city—a dream buried beneath years of muddy floors, oily utensils, and the quiet resistance of village life.

But dreams in a woman's hands can scare the ones around her.

Her father said no.

The village whispered: *"If she leaves, she will forget us."*
The grandmother muttered: *"Women don't need ambition. Their place is here."*
Her father feared more than just her absence—he feared her growth.

Still, the winds of support rose. Her maternal relatives spoke up. They reminded her father that financial hardship was already gnawing at their door. They said, *"Let her go. Let her try."* And with a heavy heart and a guarded mind, he agreed.

For months, Lily's mother would travel from her childhood home to the training center, while Lily remained in the village, learning how to pretend that everything was fine.

When the village school finally closed for summer, a new journey began. The family—just the four of them now—moved to the city.

Not everyone was happy. Her cousins, especially the elder brother who once slept beside her in the mud house, felt betrayed. *"Why didn't you take us with you?"* they asked. But the truth was simple: they could barely carry themselves. There was no room for guilt inside empty pockets.

The city was crowded and loud. The buildings looked like they had swallowed the sky, and the roads hummed with urgency. Her mother, now a trainee teacher with a modest stipend, would wear her sari like armor and leave early every morning. Her father found a small job—his hands once rough with village soil now dealt with machinery and harsh words.

Lily and her brother were admitted to different schools.

That separation cut her deeper than she could express. They had always studied together, shared lunch, whispered secrets between notebooks. Now, she stood in a school corridor alone—her brother in another building across town.

And the language.

Oh, the language. Hindi twisted her tongue. English mocked her silence.

In class, she sat near the window, eyes fixed on the sky, hoping it would offer a sentence she could understand. The girls around her giggled, wearing bows too clean, shoes too polished. Lily's hands still remembered the feel of village earth, her uniform slightly faded, her notebooks written in shaky Hindi.

And then began the cruelty.

Each day, her world grew quieter, but her mind louder.

She missed her brother's hand during lunchtime.

She missed the mud house, where dreams may have been

small but safe.
She missed the sound of her mother's soft voice teaching by lantern light.

But most of all, she missed feeling unafraid.

And so, Lily became her own shelter.

She stopped expecting others to protect her.
She picked up the pieces of her hurt and began turning them into art.
Each cruel word, each ignored plea—she stored them not in anger, but in pages and paint.

Because deep inside her, Lily knew something no one else seemed to notice—

That the girl no one protected...
Was learning how to become the woman who would protect herself.

FOUR

THE SILENCE BETWEEN WORDS

The world moved fast, too sharp, too loud,
While she stood still, beneath a cloud.
With books in hand and words unsaid,
She fought her wars inside her head.
In rooms where echoes knew her name,
But no one came… but no one came.

When they moved to the city, the air felt different—dense, restless. Buildings stretched like strangers who didn't smile, and the streets had no memory of the mud roads Lily once danced on. The sky, once so close above her village home, now felt like it belonged to someone else.

Her mother called it a new beginning.
To Lily, it felt more like an ending.

They stayed at a rented home—its walls thin, its windows tired. The landlord, a distant acquaintance, had a granddaughter named Rama. She was Lily's age. There was comfort in that. Two quiet souls met at the edge of chaos, and for a while, they walked into school each morning like a pair of whispered prayers.

Their hands held the same notebooks. Their eyes searched for the same answers. They sat side by side, laughed in soft voices, and shared secrets wrapped in biscuits and broken pencils.

But city schools had rules written in concrete. When too many children came, the walls separated them. Rama was sent to Section A. Lily remained in Section B.

And just like that... the silence returned.

The girls in her new section wore glitter in their hair and English on their tongues. Their laughter was sharp. Their shoes made no sound, but their judgment did. Lily, in her simple ribbons and stitched-up uniform, stood like a misplaced shadow.

She didn't know how to step into their circle. She didn't know how to pretend.

At lunch, she would still look for Rama—her only anchor—but slowly even Rama began to drift. New friendships, new games, new languages. Lily began to sit alone, biting her food and her feelings. The friend who once shared her lunchbox now smiled from afar with someone else.

Still, Lily kept quiet. That's what kind girls do.

Then came the day that broke the little thread she was holding on to.

She had missed an English class test. A family event in the village pulled them away, but her father promised the teacher she would write it later. Lily, nervous but obedient, stood outside the staff room when she returned, holding her notebook like a shield.

The English teacher handed her a question paper—handwritten, cold.
"Start writing," she said.

No explanation. No kindness.

Lily didn't understand. The questions felt foreign, the blanks stared like open wounds. Her hands shook as she scribbled—guessing meanings, drawing from fading memories of dusty village classrooms.

The teacher, noticing her confusion, didn't ask.
She shouted.
In front of everyone.

"Don't you even know how to read English?"

The words hit harder than slaps. Lily froze. Her legs trembled. Her face turned pale.

All she wanted to say was: *"I tried."*
But no one listens when a shy girl whispers.

She was sent upstairs and told to call a girl named Diya to the staff room.

When she reached the classroom, another teacher was already teaching. Lily hesitated. Should she interrupt? Should she speak?
Her throat closed. She quietly returned to her seat.

In the next period, the math teacher—stern and unfamiliar—asked,
"Diya, why didn't you go? Didn't someone tell you?"

"No one told me," Diya replied.

And then the finger pointed.
"She told you," said the teacher, looking straight at Lily.

In front of the entire class, Lily was asked to stand.

"You made up a story? You're lying now? You spoiled Diya's name! You didn't even do your job properly!"

What Lily didn't know—what made the pain deeper—was that this math teacher was Diya's mother.

So the scolding came not from discipline, but from pride. And the words weren't just corrections—they were wounds.

Lily's eyes welled up. Her lips didn't move. She couldn't even say sorry—because she hadn't done anything wrong.

But who would believe a girl who spoke so little?

She was told to sit.

Her body obeyed.

Her heart did not.

That night, no one at home asked why her eyes were red. She wrapped herself in her favorite blanket, hugging it like a friend that still remembered her name. She didn't cry loudly. She just let her pillow taste her tears.

She thought:

Why do people shout without listening?

Why do people judge without knowing?

Why does kindness feel like weakness in this world?

And then she whispered into the dark:

"Maybe I'm not meant to belong here."

FIVE

THORNS IN THE GARDEN

She walked through corridors lined with gold,
While her slippers whispered stories untold.
Their laughter rang like knives in air,
But no one stopped. No one cared.
And in that noise, so harsh and loud,
She wore her silence like a shroud.

Days turned into weeks, but Lily's heart remained fixed in that staff room—among the voices that scolded without asking, among the glares that dismissed her pain. But life, as always, kept moving, and Lily had no choice but to walk behind it.

At school, the walls that should've protected her became her quiet enemies. The girls in Section B weren't just strangers anymore—they were shadows that followed her.

They were rich girls. Daughters of men in suits and women who wore perfume even to the market. They never came to school alone. Drivers dropped them off. Their tiffin's smelled like cafes. Their English came out like music from polished throats.

To Lily, they felt like another world—one she wasn't invited into.

At first, they ignored her. Then they began noticing her shyness, her hesitation, her silence.

And that's when it began.

After class, they would walk past her desk and knock her books down—like it was part of a game. Sometimes, they'd laugh and mimic her accent in front of others, twisting her quiet voice into something shameful.

"Why do you talk like that?"
"Don't you know English, gaav ki chhori?"
"Look at her hair—she still braids like a village girl!"

They began untying her braids, letting them fall like unwelcome roots in a city garden. And when she bent down to tie them again, one of them would flick her ear or tug her ribbon.

She never fought back. Not because she didn't want to—but because she didn't know how.

One day, they surrounded her in the corridor after class.

"Let's play a game," one said.
"Close your eyes and stand still."

Lily, not understanding, obeyed—thinking maybe, just maybe, they were being friendly today.

But the moment she closed her eyes, something hit her back. Then another. Then laughter.

She opened her eyes to see bits of paper, pencil shavings, a half-eaten biscuit tossed at her feet.

"You're too dumb to play anyway," one girl smirked.

The laughter echoed in her ears all the way home.

That evening, Lily tried telling her parents.

"Bas kuch nahi, wo thoda majak karte hain," she said softly, not wanting to sound like a complaint.

Her mother looked tired, cooking on a kerosene stove. Her father didn't even glance up from the newspaper.

"Rich kids just show off," he said. "Ignore them. Don't make it a big deal."

That's all they said. That's all.

No one thought it was cruelty. No one saw it was bullying.

Lily understood then: when people believe your pain isn't big enough, you have to carry it alone.

She stopped mentioning school after that.

The next day, and the one after that, the bullying continued—soft, hidden, cruel. They would take her eraser, push her gently so she stumbled, whisper things behind her back that made others laugh.

Sometimes, she cried quietly in the bathroom, wiping her eyes with the end of her dupatta, praying no one would walk in.

Other times, she just smiled at the wall—pretending she was somewhere else, maybe back in her village, under the neem tree where she once painted flowers on stones.

But one thing she never did... was stop going.

Lily kept showing up.

Even with her heart aching and eyes heavy, even with a fear of what new insult would come next, she tied her braids, packed her bag, and walked into school.

Because deep inside her, something still believed—

One day, the world will learn to see beyond the shine.

One day, someone will hear her story before judging her silence.

SIX

THE EVENING SHADOWS NEVER LEFT

In the hush of twilight's fading breath,
She walked with steps that carried death.
Not the kind that stops a heart—
But the one that tears a soul apart.
The world went on, no voices rose,
Only her fear in silence froze.
And from that day till all her years,
She walked alone... with unseen tears.

The city had a strange silence in the evenings—
a silence not of peace, but of doors that closed early,
of lights that flickered behind curtains,
of fear disguised as routine.

Lily had started attending a new school now—
co-ed, unlike the last.
Her brother was there too, but in a different class,
and different in more ways than one.

He was changing.
Rougher. Sharper.
Not cruel, but cracked in his own hidden corners.
Maybe the world had taught him that softness was
dangerous.
Maybe, like her,
he too was learning to survive in a place
that did not honour kindness.

They walked to school together—
though 'together' was a fragile word.
He always walked ahead,
his feet faster, his fearless stride
leaving Lily behind to guess when to cross the road,
her little hands trembling, eyes darting.
She didn't know how to navigate traffic.
He never waited.
And she… she never asked him to.

One evening, the world shifted.
Her mother had asked her to fetch a notebook—
a simple errand,
but dusk was already leaning toward darkness.

Lily and her friend from the apartment went out,
bare feet echoing on the tiled floor of fear.
They returned,
only to find the wrong size.
Her mother handed her the notebook back and said—
"Go change it."
Just like that.
No second thought.
No second glance.

So Lily went.
Alone.

The streets were quiet.
The sky was a soft bruise of violet and smoke.
And as she walked back—
a man appeared.
Middle-aged. On a cycle.
A stranger with something familiar in his cruelty.
He stopped her.
Words weren't needed—his hands spoke instead.
One gripped her wrist.
The other... wandered.
She wanted to scream.
But silence had lived in her throat for years.
So she begged God without words.
Tears blurred her vision.
She froze—until something inside her cracked open.
"Run."
Her legs flew.
Her heart pounded in every step.
She darted through alleys,
passing closed doors and closed worlds.
In her village, doors were always open.
But here, in the city—
everything was locked.
Even hearts.
She reached home, breathless,
as if chased by hell itself.
She sobbed.
Her mother told her to wash her hands.
Her father shouted.
Not at the man.
At her mother.
In the morning,
he spoke to the landlord.

The old man said—
"You're from a village. Don't make it a big deal."
    And that was that.
Her story ended at someone else's comfort.
No one said, *"I believe you."*
No one said, *"I'm sorry this happened."*
They said, *"Be careful next time."*
    That night became a before and after.
    A few days later,
she and her brother were invited to a neighbour's home—
for halwa.
A treat.
A small joy.
    When it was time to return,
darkness had already arrived,
soft and dangerous.
    Her brother ran ahead again,
as always.
Free from fear.
But she—
she was still a prisoner of it.
    The neighbour's husband offered to walk her home.
She refused.
Terrified.
Every man was now a storm in disguise.
She ran.
Faster than her breath could catch up.
Across roads.
Through fear.
    The man followed—
not to harm her,
but to protect her.
Still, she didn't believe in protection anymore.

She reached home,
a wild mess of fear and sweat.
Her heart thundered.
The man arrived behind her, concerned.
    And yet again—
her parents scolded her.
    "She's mad."
"What's wrong with her?"
    But no one asked—
"What happened to her?"
    No one saw that a little girl's world
had burned in silence.
    She never went out alone again.
She stopped laughing without reason.
She stopped trusting light.
And she stopped believing that safety
was a right given to girls.
    In her little diary, she wrote one line:
"I am afraid of men. Even if they smile."
    She was only nine.
    And a part of her—
never came home that night.
    She was just nine, with trembling hands,
Facing a world she couldn't understand.
A monster's grip, a doorless night,
Yet in her fear, she chose to fight.
    No knights arrived, no hero came,
But still she walked through fire and flame.
And though her voice was never loud,
She broke the silence, bruised but proud.
    Now when the wind whispers her name,
It carries echoes, not of shame.
But of a girl who still walks through fear—

With haunted steps, yet crystal clear.

SEVEN

THE DOLL THAT SANG GOODBYE

"She held the sky in her small soft palms,
A doll, a plate, a teacup calm.
Little joys she stitched with thread,
Of silence, pain no one ever read."

In the blurred timeline of Lily's shifting childhood, when city after city and rented home after home kept changing like seasons, she once found solace in a neighbourly bond. A kind-hearted Didi, lived next door in one of the rented lanes. Lily would often return from school and spend the quiet afternoons with her, sharing the warmth of borrowed sisterhood. Didi fed her lovingly, laughed with her, and once, gave her something that etched itself into Lily's fragile memory — a tiny crockery miniature tea set. Cup and plate for chai — a child's world of elegance and joy. It was the first gift Lily had ever received in her life.

She held that gift with the reverence a queen might give her crown. It was not just crockery; it was love moulded into shape — her first sense of being thought of, remembered. For a girl who had rarely asked for anything, who had learned to bite her lips instead of crying when needs were not met, the miniature set became her treasure.

Another memory, stitched with faded pink and faded pain, emerged from the folds of her heart — the plastic doll. But it was not hers by birth. It had first belonged to her brother, the first child of the family. It had long been hidden away by her maternal grandmother, stored in a box with the hope of giving it someday to grandchildren who weren't even born yet. One day, Lily saw it when the box was opened. She was instantly drawn to it — not because it sang, for it had stopped singing by then — but because it was beautiful, and it was the only toy she had ever longed for.

At first, her grandmother refused. She said it was not meant for her. But Lily insisted, gently at first, then with tears. Her soft pleading reached the ears of her grandfather, who quietly sent the doll to Lily through her mother. And just like that, it became hers. Her first real toy — something that finally belonged to her.

She took care of it as if it were made of glass. She dressed it, tucked it in, spoke to it. Her world became gentler when that doll was nearby. But the sweetness was short-lived. One day, a cousin who often came by with mischief in her eyes, broke the doll's leg while playing. Lily didn't scream. She sat in a quiet corner, wrapping the broken limb in transparent tape, whispering apologies to her silent friend.

But change came knocking again. They were shifting homes once more. Her father, weary of clutter and sentiment, told her plainly, "What will you do with this broken doll? Give it to the neighbour's daughter. They're younger, they'll play with it."

Lily froze. Her heart clutched at the doll as if it could save her from all the moving, all the leaving. But she was told — "You are big now." So, she gave it away. No tantrum. No drama. Just an invisible heartbreak. The kind she was getting used to.

In their new home, nestled in another crowded lane, a little boy saw Lily playing with her precious miniature tea set — the one Didi had gifted her. He reached out for it with sparkling eyes, and his mother simply said, "Give it to him, beta. He's younger. You're big now."

Lily was only ten.

Only ten — and already expected to let go. Already expected to be the bigger person. She gave it, hands trembling, eyes watering. Another goodbye. Another piece of herself handed over in silence.

That night, she cried again. Not just because she lost a toy. But because no one saw that she needed love too. She wanted to be the little one, just once. To be protected. To be allowed to hold something and say — this is mine.

But her voice had been trained to say yes. Trained to nod. To obey. To give up and grow up. And somewhere in that soft, tender space where childhood once lived, Lily began to disappear. Bit by bit.

This chapter in Lily's life was the quiet birthplace of a pattern: of sacrifices stitched in silence. Of a girl who learned to give up pieces of herself without ever being asked how it felt. It seemed so small — a doll, a tea set — yet it was the beginning of an emotional erosion. The rise of a girl who learned to be quiet, learned to please, learned to nod... even when her heart said no.

As she grew older, in real life challenges, Lily often struggled to say no. Not because she didn't want to — but because somewhere deep inside her, a little girl's voice still echoed, *"You're big now... give it away."* That lesson, embedded early in her soul, left a scar. She became the girl who couldn't refuse, who sacrificed her comfort, peace, even dreams — all to be the good one.

And somewhere deep inside, the echo of that long-broken doll still lived...

"Happy birthday... happy..."

But it no longer sang for her.

"She gave away her teacups,
She gave away her song,
She gave away her little joys,
To prove she could be strong.

But in the silence of her soul, _
A cry was buried low —
Not every girl who smiles wide
Is ready yet to grow." _

EIGHT

THE GREEN BOX OF LOVE

They laughed at the box, not knowing its flame,
A soap tin packed with a father's name.
Roti folded like soft-spoken love,
And sabzi stirred with care from above.
It wasn't the box, but what it contained—
A moment of kindness that quietly remained.

City schools were nothing like the ones Lily had known in her little village. Here, children flaunted tiffin boxes shaped like cartoon characters, some even had separate compartments for fruits and desserts. The air buzzed with branded lunch bags and color-coded water bottles, every item carrying a story of money, not memory.

That day, Lily went to school carrying last night's roti and a tiny smear of mango pickle, carefully wrapped by her mother in the early glow of dawn. Her mother was neck-deep in her training, preparing for an exam that might change everything for the family. Cooking a fresh lunch wasn't possible. Still, Lily never complained. Her heart had grown used to the rhythm of silence.

At lunchtime, an unexpected announcement echoed in the corridor.

"Lily and her brother, your tiffin box has arrived. Please collect it from the gate."

She exchanged a confused glance with her brother. They had already brought their food. But curiosity nudged them to the school gate.

There, in the hands of the school guard, lay a box—a bright green plastic container. But not just any box.

It was a dishwashing soap box. The kind used to scrub utensils at home.

A white paper was glued to the lid, their names written in bold ink, curling slightly at the edges where the adhesive failed. Inside it—hot, soft rotis and a fragrant potato sabzi. Still steaming.

Their father had come, sometime mid-morning. He had noticed that the children had carried only last night's leftovers. And something in him stirred.

He had rolled out fresh rotis on the iron tawa with trembling hands, cutting the potatoes like they were precious, seasoning them not with just spices but with guilt and love and an apology only a parent can offer without words.

Lily could feel it. With every bite she took, she could feel the weight of his effort, and the warmth of those rotis melted her heart.

But inside the classroom, laughter spread like spilled ink.

"What is this? A soap box?"

"Do you wash dishes or eat lunch?"

"Is that sabzi or soap?"

Lily sat silently. Her head bent. Her eyes moist. The box was green, old, with scratches. But what it held—was not just food. It was a father's trembling attempt to nourish his children, to show them love in the only language he knew—actions.

She didn't cry in front of them. She simply held the spoon tighter and whispered to her soul:

"Let them laugh. They will never know the taste of this kind of love."

Her father—often strict, often distant—had done something no one else had. He had chosen care over ego. In his small, silent way.

That day, Lily learned that sometimes the most beautiful emotions come wrapped in the ugliest boxes. And that real nourishment isn't shaped by plastic colors or lunchbox brands.

It is shaped by love.

They carried steel, I carried pain,
They mocked my box, again and again.
But in that soap-scratched plastic hue,
Was something richer than their view.
My father's fingers, flour-dust kissed,
His silent love I almost missed.
No silver fork, no designer tray—
But food made love me anyway.

NINE

FOOTPRINTS IN FLEETING SANDS

They say she's shy, too quiet to shine,
But silent stars still light the sky.
She walks alone through winters deep,
Holding the dreams she dares not speak.
And every time she starts to stay,
Life whispers, "No, it's time to stray."

The town was not quite a village, not quite a city—a space in between, like Lily herself, caught between silence and unspoken dreams. Her mother's new posting brought them to this half-city, half-village land where the local language danced in the air like dust caught in afternoon sunbeams. Here, Lily tried to live quietly, gently, the way flowers lean into morning light. She made a few friends—only girls, of course—she had always been afraid of boys. They played simple games, shared school lunches, and for a while, Lily felt a flicker of something soft and close to happy.

But even joy had its cost.

When the school announced a 3000-meter walk tournament, Lily's heart stammered. This was her first journey away from home, her very first experience without the presence of her mother or father. The tournament required her to stay near the school for three whole days. The boys and girls were to go together, with teachers, but Lily had never known such freedom. Her father, often strict and skeptical, would never allow her to travel alone. Yet this time, he said yes.

Perhaps it was fate. Or perhaps the universe, in some rare mercy, had decided she deserved to feel strong.

She practiced daily for it—rising with the freezing breath of winter mornings, walking with cold feet and trembling fingers, coming back again in the fading golden hours of evening. She did not know how to pronounce her own name with confidence, but she walked with everything she had. Her teachers mocked her; one said, "How can she go to a science fair? She can't even speak her name." Others would whisper, "She's from the city, but she's still like a village girl. So quiet. So slow."

They laughed. But Lily kept walking.

She walked in silence, through judgment and jokes, through tired legs and trembling fears. And at the end, she won a medal.

But it wasn't just the medal that mattered. It was the quiet victory of standing on a stage, trembling inside but not fleeing. It was the warmth of her friends' cheers. And it was the truth that even if no teacher believed in her, even if her voice was too soft, her steps had strength. She returned, medal in hand, and her school hosted Sports Day. There she played cricket, and games she didn't even know the names of. She laughed. She ran. She shone—for a moment.

Then, change came again.

Her mother's transfer orders arrived, and they had to move again—to a new city, a new school, a new beginning. The old friends were left behind like pressed flowers in a forgotten book. Lily cried. Of course she cried. But no one asked her if she was okay. No one asked if she was ready.

And this pattern, it carved itself into her heart.

Even before, in that same town, her father had enrolled her in a tuition class where the head teacher said cruel things like, "You should be smarter, louder, like the other girls. You live in a city, why do you still talk like a village girl?" But he didn't know—no one knew—how many homes she had left behind. How many times she'd had to start again.

In that little town, Lily had performed in her first-ever school tableau. She'd stood there, dressed in borrowed clothes, heart pounding, yet glowing in the thrill of being seen. But it didn't last. Again, they moved. Again, she was expected to smile, adjust, forget.

How could she attach herself to anyone when she knew everything would be taken away? Why make friends when they'd become memories too soon? Her soft heart couldn't harden like others. It bled quietly.

She feared attachment, not because she didn't crave love, but because life had taught her it came with loss. Every smile risked a tear. Every hand held would one day wave goodbye. So she stayed quiet. She stayed careful.

Lily—the girl who learned from pain, who grew in silence, who walked 3000 meters not just on a field but through every shadow that told her she wasn't enough.

I stitched a medal to my chest,
Not just of gold, but all the rest—
Of mornings cold and voices cruel,
Of trying hard in every school.

Of friends I made and had to leave,
Of dreams I dared but couldn't grieve.
I fear the bond, the touch, the thread,
For every love has always fled.
But still I walk, though not too fast,
And carry ghosts from every past.
Someday, perhaps, I'll call it grace—
This fragile soul in borrowed place.

TEN

THE SUMMER THAT NEVER CAME AGAIN

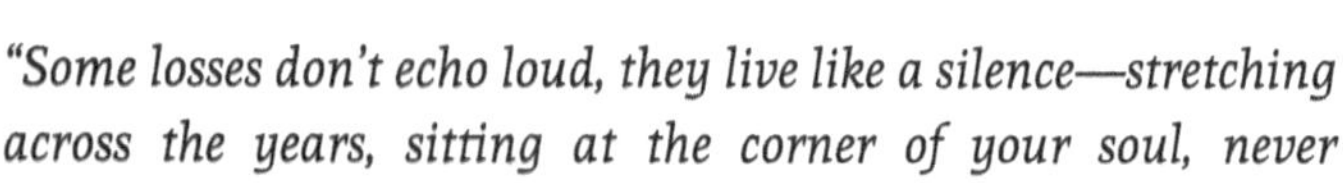

"Some losses don't echo loud, they live like a silence—stretching across the years, sitting at the corner of your soul, never leaving."

Lily was eighteen now, but there were parts of her that would forever be frozen in the summer of her childhood—the summer that never came again.

There was someone—someone more than just a sister. Her cousin, her didi, her only friend since childhood. Not just a person, but a feeling, a presence, a safe place wrapped in laughter, secrets, and whispered dreams. Every year, like clockwork, Lily would wait for summer vacations, not because of the heat or freedom, but because her didi would come. And with her, came joy.

But one Sunday, joy never arrived.

It was supposed to be a regular day. Lily had her practical exams. Her didi asked her to come along somewhere that morning. Lily, worried about the exam, gently said no.

She never got another chance to say yes.

That same day, her didi was gone.

No farewell. No last hug. Just gone.

The house felt heavier that day, like it knew something Lily didn't. The silence wasn't empty—it screamed. The news shattered her. The world spun, but she stood still. Grief didn't knock. It stormed in. Her heart cracked like an old wall, and something inside slipped through—a soundless scream.

Her didi—the one who gifted her the first keypad phone, who knew all her secrets, who always said, *"Tu meri sabse pyaari behen hai"*—was now just a memory. That phone, once hidden in her school bag on silent mode for safety, now lay in a drawer like a relic of lost love.

Her didi had protected her from boys, from the world, from fear. She knew every shade of Lily's innocence. They shared a language of glances and giggles, of untold pain, of unspoken strength. Now there was no one left to speak that language with.

Lily cried for months. Not loud, but deep. The kind of crying that hollowed out your chest. The kind that turned her quiet.

She never went back to that village. The summer vacation never returned. Because her didi wasn't there, and neither was Lily. Not the same Lily, at least.

And slowly, something else grew inside her—a fear. A fear of losing the people she loved. If someone didn't return a call. If someone came home late. If someone left without a goodbye. Her heart clenched in silent panic. She had learned too early that love could be taken without warning.

Why did God write her story like this? Why must the softest hearts be tested the hardest?

The world around her moved on. But Lily—she carried her didi in her silences, in her aching chest, in every summer breeze.

She had learned to smile with pain tucked underneath.

She had learned that people don't just die—they take parts of you with them.

And still, she rose.

But the summer never came again.

Yet in the quiet echoes of her didi's absence, something gentle grew. Lily had watched her sister stitch beauty into torn fabrics and craft magic out of waste. Her didi's fingers moved like poetry—turning scraps into stories, meals into memories. She was an unbelievable cook, the kind who didn't follow recipes, but followed her heart. The aroma of her food lingered like love in the walls.

Lily remembered every fold, every thread, every spice.

And unknowingly, as the seasons passed, she began to mirror her. Bit by bit, day by day, she picked up the needle, the scissors, the ladle. She stitched when her heart ached. She cooked when words failed. She made beauty from brokenness.

Perhaps, it was her didi's way of still being with her—in her hands, in her habits, in her art.

Because love, when deep enough, never really dies.

"The Summer She Took With Her"

She came with June, like sunshine soft, With anklets' chime and laughter loft. Each year I'd wait, heart in bloom, For her to fill the silent room.

But one warm day, the light turned grey, And joy just packed its bags away. I stayed behind, with words unsaid, While summer turned to grief instead.

She held my secrets in her palms, She calmed my storms with silent calms. Now every breeze that strokes my hair, Whispers her name, and she's not there.

She was my sister, soul, and shield, The heart I wore but never healed. A single 'no' became my scar— A moment's choice that traveled far.

The world moved on—but I did not, Each clock tick tangled in a knot. For grief is not what poems pretend, It's waking where a story ends.

So now I sit where summers fade, With love unspent and debts unpaid. I loved her more than I could show— And summers now just come and go.

But in my chest, she lives so wide— A tender ghost I cannot hide. And every time the warm winds stir... I wait again... for the summer that came with her.

ELEVEN

THE PATH SHE NEVER CHOSE, YET WALKED

"Not every dream dies with thunder. Some dissolve slowly, like sugar in tea—leaving behind a strange, silent sweetness and ache."

Lily was healing, gently. One breath at a time. One day at a time.

But life wasn't waiting.

The day finally came when she had to step out again—to college. The dream she held close since she was a child—the dream to become a doctor—was slowly fading before her eyes. She could barely pronounce the word back then, always saying *"dactni"* when someone asked, *"What do you want to become when you grow up?"* Her eyes sparkled with certainty. Her heart knew.

But certainty was never enough.

Her parents never really believed she could do it. Not because they didn't love her, but because she was always 'average'—not extraordinary, not a topper, not the kind to be expected to carry a stethoscope one day. Her brother, the intelligent one, had always been their hope, their pride.

For Lily, passing the 12th board itself was the ceiling they set for her.

So, when the time came to fill the entrance exam form, she hesitated. Her mother said softly, *"If you're truly prepared, go ahead. But we don't have that kind of money right now."*

And just like that, her dream dissolved.

Her brother prepared for two years. She did not. She wasn't allowed to. It wasn't anyone's fault, not hers, not theirs. But the pain sat quietly inside her chest like a sealed envelope that no one cared to open.

She got admitted into a government college for B.Sc. A co-ed college. Her first. After years in a girls' school, it was like stepping into a different universe.

The day she returned home from admission, she broke down in her mother's lap, trembling, *"There are so many boys, Maa. I don't know how to be around boys."*

Childhood trauma still lived inside her like a shadow.

Her mother calmed her gently, *"Just don't talk to them. Do your work. Don't worry."*

So she did.

Lily became the girl who never asked for help. The girl who finished every practical and theory on her own. Other girls whispered sweetly to boys to get their files done. Some girls were charming, strategic. Lily wasn't.

She kept her distance. She didn't go out to eat pani patasha after college, didn't go shopping with them, didn't join laughter-filled selfies. Something inside her said—*They won't stay. They'll only take what they want.*

One day, during an exam, a girl copied answers from Lily's sheet. Later, that same girl mocked Lily in front of others, *"That's the answer I gave. You know, I told her the correct one."* Lily had stayed up the whole night to memorize those answers. Her kindness had become someone else's crown.

She felt anger, confusion, sorrow—all tucked behind a forced smile. She wanted to scream. To tell the teacher. To speak up. But she didn't know how.

She never had.

The semester passed. Then the years. She completed her graduation. Her heart still ached for the dreams she never lived.

She wanted to pursue M.Sc. in Zoology but couldn't get a seat.

Then one day, she heard about a Postgraduate Diploma in Dietetics being offered by a government university in her city. Twenty seats. That was all.

She enrolled.

That year, her family finally shifted to a permanent home in the same city where she had studied from class 10 onwards. No more packing. No more decorating just to leave it all behind. This home was hers.

She painted the walls with her memories, hung her art like healing, arranged each corner with her hands—the hands that once held grief like glass.

In that university, she didn't make real friends. Just classmates. Acquaintances. Safe distances.

She traveled every day, two autos each way, carrying her dreams and her silence.

Then, just before the diploma ended, the pandemic arrived.

Online classes began. The world closed. But something opened for Lily.

One day, her brother told her about a Master's degree—offered in a medical college, a rare course not many knew about. He was pursuing his own medical diploma and thought she could try.

She hesitated.

Me? In a medical college? The same girl who once said *dactni?*

But this time, she chose to try.

She gave the entrance exam. And while the results were yet to come, her diploma ended. She waited in the silence between two dreams.

Some people have smooth roads. Lily had pebbles.

She had faced a world that didn't hold her hand. She had smiled through betrayals, helped people who never thanked her, held secrets that no one asked about. She had grown up too soon. Her childhood dreams were edited by reality. But still, she didn't break.

Because even the softest petals learn how to bloom in stone.

This was her beginning—not of a girl who got everything. But of a girl who gave everything... and still stood tall.

"For the Dreams That Stayed Inside"

They asked me once, *what will you be?* I smiled and said, *"a dactni."* The word was crooked, soft and small— But dreams don't care for speech at all.

I grew, but dreams grew slower still, Behind the walls of 'can't' and 'will.' They gave my brother stars to chase, And left me with a smaller space.

I watched the world from cornered eyes, Where silence was my best disguise. They said I'm sweet, they took my hand, But used me more than they could stand.

My kindness turned to quiet ache, My voice a road I could not take. They copied answers, claimed my truth, And mocked the labor of my youth.

I cried in halls I could not leave, I smiled through every quiet grieve. I held my dreams like folded lace, And wore my shyness on my face.

But now I walk with heavier feet, Through shifting homes and silent streets. Yet in my palms, I hold a flame, A soft, strange hope I cannot name.

A house is mine. A wall, a light. I paint my past in colors bright. No stethoscope—yet something new, A path that somehow feels more true.

And though the world once shut its door, I found another, something more. So here I stand—not loud, but clear, Still walking, though the dream's not near.

I never screamed. I never told. But I grew roots inside the cold. And now, though shy, I start to rise— With quiet fire behind my eyes.

TWELVE

THE GIRL WHO WALKED THROUGH FIRE

"Some girls are made of petals and prayers.
Others are carved from storms and silent screams.
And some, like Lily—
are built from broken pieces stitched with hope."

There was a time Lily couldn't step outside alone.

Now she lived miles away from home—in a strange city, among strangers, surviving... not just surviving, but *living*.

But this ending wasn't soft.
It was born from ashes.

She had cried the night her master's result came—not from failure, but from fear. Fear of distance. Of the unknown. A new city. No friends. No one to guide her.

For a while, it felt like the world was mocking her bravery.

She was the only one selected in her course. One seat. No batchmates. Just her—and a male senior.

Her heart panicked.

She had never spoken to boys in college. Now, her only guide was someone she feared to even greet. She stayed quiet, shrinking, scared of making mistakes—until life gave her no choice but to speak. And she did. With trembling words and a shaky voice—but she did.

In the medical institute, seniors weren't mentors. They were bosses.

The rules were unwritten, the help was missing.

Lily learned not from lectures, but from silence.

At first, she was treated like furniture—asked to type schedules, print papers, paste posters, manage work no one else wanted.

She cried at night. Not because the work was too much, but because *no one saw her.*

She was just... there.

And then came the seminars.

The girl who once couldn't answer roll call now had to speak in front of professors, experts, seniors.

She studied all night, trembling with fear.

A faculty said out loud,

"She can't do it. She doesn't even know how to speak."

She swallowed her tears—and proved them wrong.

Her seminar was so good that the same people who doubted her claimed credit.

She smiled, not because it didn't hurt—

But because **she knew now what she was capable of.**

Still, she sat alone in her room most days.

Still, they used her for tasks others refused.

Still, she wasn't taught—just *used.*

Then came the crushing news.

A council rule.

Her degree would no longer count.

No jobs. No future. Just a paper.

Seniors said, *"Quit."*

But Lily had no backup. No rich family. No second chances.

She cried again. Not because she was weak.

But because the **world was cruel to those who didn't fight back**.

Still, she stayed.

She kept showing up. Through insults, work politics, and loneliness.

She didn't butter anyone. She didn't manipulate.

She just... *endured*.

Some months passed.

COVID took over the world.

Transport stopped. Her father and brother dropped her to college every day.

Then she learned to ride a scooty.

Rain. Roads. Wind. Freedom.

For the first time in her life, she felt wings on her back.

And then, somehow—life moved.

She completed her research. Passed her final exam.

The world still questioned her degree, but she knew what it had cost her. She knew what it had taught her.

She applied for PhD. Got selected.

Under the same supervisor.

In the same place that bruised her soul.

She said no.

She wasn't the same scared Lily anymore.

Then came a job offer. Far away. Another city. Another life.

Her father hesitated. Her mother held her hand. Her brother pushed her forward.

And she went.

She, who once cried over a city two hours away—
Now lived in a new state,
Worked in a respected institute,
Earned a salary,
And funded her dreams.
She paid her bills. She made her tea. She walked alone.
And every time the night felt too long, she whispered,
"I made it this far. I won't stop now."
She didn't just grow up—
She *rose*.
From the mud of her village to the halls of a medical college,
From silent breakdowns to brave seminars,
From doubting herself to inspiring others—
Lily became her own miracle.

"The Fire Did Not Burn Her"

They said,
"She can't survive.
She doesn't know the way."
But Lily walked through shadows
That never saw the day.

They gave her work, not wisdom,
Silence, not a hand.
She cried into her pillow
When no one could understand.

They mocked her broken language,
They laughed behind closed doors.
She stood—still soft, still shaking—
Yet stronger than before.

They changed the rules midway,
Said her dreams were out of place.
But how do you stop a storm
That's learned to dance with grace?

She learned to ride in rain,
To cook, to speak, to fall.
She lost her faith, then found it
Inside herself, after all.

They'll never know the nights
She wept and wiped her face.
But Lily, made of lightning—
She never left the race.

A girl no one believed in
Now stands with lifted chin.
The world tried hard to break her...
But Lily chose to win.

The End... or perhaps, the beginning.

She is not just a girl anymore.
She is a lighthouse.
For every Lily who's still afraid, still unseen, still unheard.
She is proof that **you can walk through fire and bloom
anyway**.

To All The Lilies Of The World

To Every Lily Who Ever Felt Alone
    Lily is no more just a character.
She is me.
I am Lily.
I wrote her story with trembling fingers and tear-soaked nights.
And now, as this final page turns, I want to tell you the truth.
    This isn't a tale spun from fantasy.
This is my life—every heartbeat of it.
My name is **Shweta**,
And Lily was the name I gave to the girl inside me
—soft, scared, but stubbornly brave—
inspired by the haunting lines of Alan Walker's song:
    "Lily was a little girl
Afraid of the big, wide world
She grew up within her castle walls..."
    Yes, I grew up within the fragile castle walls of expectations, poverty, silence, and scars.
But *then she ran.*
And so did I—
Away from fears,
Away from suffocating norms,
Towards dreams,
Even if my feet bled,
Even if the road ahead was lonely.
    I walked alone through shadows,
Fell in classrooms filled with silence,
Broke under the weight of expectations,
And rose quietly—
again, and again,

because I had no one to carry me—
except the little Lily inside.

The **backcover page** of this book, the painting you saw first,
is also painted by Lily—by me.
A silent brush in a loud world.
Colours I never spoke, but poured onto paper.

To every girl who reads this—
who cried silently in her room,
who buried her voice in classrooms,
who did her best and was told it wasn't enough,
who fought with empty pockets and full hearts,
I see you.
I am you.

You don't need a prince to rescue you—
You are the girl with the sword in her own story.
To every Lily walking this big, cruel world alone—
I want to hug you tight.
Because I know. I *know*.

This book is my soul spilled out.
It's every moment I doubted myself.
Every time someone said I wasn't enough.
And still, I stayed. I studied. I worked. I healed.
I became the woman I needed as a girl.

To my mother and brother—
your belief made me breathe.
To those few who stood by me—
thank you, for being the flicker of light
when my world went dark.

And now, before I close,
let me leave behind a poem
—for you, dear reader,
and for the Lily within you—

A Whisper Named Lily

Enter Caption

"A Whisper Named Lily"

She wasn't made of thunder,
Nor stars that blaze and burn—
She was the quiet whisper
That begged the world to turn.

She cried in painted corners,
With pencils, words, and skies,
And from her broken silence
A thousand dreams would rise.

She wasn't made for marble,
But mud and smoke and scars,
Yet still she built a castle
And counted hope as stars.

They tried to dim her daylight,
Dismiss her without name,
But oh, she learned to shimmer
Through ridicule and shame.

A girl afraid of voices,
Now sings beneath the sun,
She is the breath of battles
That quietly are won.

So if you're lost and hurting,
And tears fall in your sleep—
Remember: **Lily's walking too**,
Where dreams and darkness meet.

With all my heart,
To all the LILIES of the world,
From the one who lived it—

—Shweta (Lily)

?

She ran away in her sleep... and dreamed of paradise.

www.ingramcontent.com/pod-product-compliance
Lightning Source LLC
Chambersburg PA
CBHW020330180726
47991CB00019B/1126